Joseph Thomas Chapman

Lyrical Poems, and Thoughts in Rhyme

Joseph Thomas Chapman

Lyrical Poems, and Thoughts in Rhyme

ISBN/EAN: 9783744788021

Printed in Europe, USA, Canada, Australia, Japan

Cover: Foto ©Andreas Hilbeck / pixelio.de

More available books at **www.hansebooks.com**

LYRICAL POEMS

THOUGHTS IN RHYME;

BY

JOSEPH THOMAS CHAPMAN.

[ENTERED AT STATIONERS' HALL.]

LONDON :
SIMPKIN, MARSHALL, & CO., STATIONERS' HALL COURT.
WESTON-SUPER-MARE :
W. H. TAYLER, PUBLIC LIBRARY, ESPLANADE AND REGENT STREET.

PREFACE.

To the innumerable persons who, like the author, have led somewhat of a double existence, engrossed for the most part in the trivial pursuits of practical life, yet wandering at times into the region of philosophical speculation, and feeling often, though but seldom and then with difficulty expressing the rapturous impulses of the poet,—many of the thoughts and emotions in the following pages, though clad in mean attire, will be familiar as old and confidential acquaintances.

Written at intervals during the leisure moments of several years, it was only natural that some diversity of style and sentiment should be exhibited. Except in the earlier pieces, the prevailing feeling which struggled for utterance was that of an overwhelming sense of human insignificance and ignorance, when compared with the infinitude above us and the positive knowledge at present beyond our reach. And whoever reflects cannot be wholly a stranger to this sentiment. For, laying aside the dreams and theories of philosophy, and assuming the existence of an outer world as it appears to us, and that sense conveys correct impressions and science is substantially true, we still find ourselves enveloped in doubt and our sources of information lamentably few. To have no means of communication with the world of immaterial spirits, and yet to believe that only a veil separates us from the unseen, and that the mysterious something we call self, if released from the material prison in which it is confined, would be capable of almost unlimited capacities of thought and emotion; and, further, even within this material universe, to be confined to one little sphere, having no means of exchanging sympathy and intelligence with the inhabitants of the innumerable other worlds in space; and even of this sphere itself to be comparatively ignorant;—all these things, when regarded alone, cannot but be humiliating to our pride and maddening to our ambition. Nor is our dissatisfaction lessened when we reflect that there appears no reason in the nature of things why death, disease, decay, excessive physical toil, with all the other ills of which we complain, should not be materially lessened or entirely removed, even without any fundamental change in our organisations and modes of existence, if we could but discover the truths that lie hidden around us. But the discontent which these reflections occasion is succeeded by hope and gratitude when we believe that all these coveted treasures of wisdom and happiness will really be acquired in future stages of our existence.

All present conceptions of the future are, however, necessarily vague and inadequate; and if, millions and millions of years hence, the spirit of the writer, in its wanderings through infinity, should meet that of some former inhabitant of earth, how contemptibly beneath the truth, in all probability, will such dreamings as those which are the subject of many of the following poems appear to have been.

JOSEPH THOMAS CHAPMAN.

CONTENTS.

CLARKE, PRINTER, "GAZETTE" OFFICE, WESTON-SUPER-MARE.

Twilight.

———

Hush ! ye winds ! the earth is sleeping !
  Speak in whispers, whisper low,
For her maids with lamps are keeping
  Anxious watch on her below.
Nurse her gently in your cradle,
  To and fro.

See ! the twilight is reposing
  On the bosom of the air,
And the lips of sound are closing,
  Save a murmur here and there,—
As the echo of the angels'
  Ev'ning prayer.

Thoughts that when the world is waking
  Vanish to a purer clime,
Now in silent waves are breaking,
  Wafted by the wings of rhyme
From the souls of loftier beings
  Into mine.

A Philosopher's Address to his Soul.

———

I live and feel, but know not why.
    I think, but know not how.
I know not what it is to die,
    Nor what my nature now.
But this I know, from some deep source
My thoughts, as rivers in their course,
    In ceaseless torrents roll.
That living spring, whose depths profound
Philosophy has failed to sound,
    I name my soul.

It is a mine of mental wealth,
    A sun to mental skies,
A universe within itself,
    A god in human guise.
Oh! tell me, thou mysterious guest
Who hold'st thy court within my breast,
    Engirt in robes of thought,
Oh, tell me what and whence thou art,
To me that glimpse of thee impart
    Which sages sought.

Did thy immortal life begin
   When nature gave me birth,—
An infant soul, and cradled in
   An infant form of earth?
Or didst thou live for countless years,
With rapture filled, in brighter spheres,
   In pure, ethereal climes?
And wert thou justly doomed to dwell
A captive in a mortal cell,
   To purge thy crimes?

Did'st thou, in gorgeous robes of state,
   O'er some fair planet reign?
And dost thou with impatience wait
   To wear those robes again?
Or wert thou once a chainless mind,
A spirit perfect, pure, refined,
   Unmixed, unclothed, unseen?
When death thy earthly sleep shall break,
Wilt thou once more a spirit wake
   From life's dull dream?

Are all my hopes, and joys, and woes
   Thy wild waves' ebb and flow?
And dost thou, ocean-like, repose
   In unknown depths below?
Are sense and science streams that glide
With nature's thoughts to swell thy tide,
   As rivers feed the sea?
There is a bound to ocean's roar,
But is there beach, or strand, or shore,
   My soul, to thee?

On life's broad flood thou art my bark,
  My future is thy freight,
But art thou sailing in the dark ?
  And is thy helmsman Fate ?
Or canst thou, in thy free career,
In spite of tide or tempest, steer
  To virtue, truth, and fame ?
Thy will thy only guiding star ?
Thyself as uncontrolled as are
  The winds and main ?

Oh tell me dost thou not at times
  In visions of the night,
Or in the poet's raptured rhymes,
  Or fancy's wildest flight,
A moment quit this form of clay,
And with the disembodied stray
  O'er earth, and sea, and sky ?
Will each remembrance that has fled,
Though now it slumbers like the dead,
  Yet never die ?

Though Nature, by her magic laws,
  Can change whate'er we see ;
Yet not an atom can she cause
  To be, or cease to be.
But when this body finds a grave,
Will dark oblivion's icy wave
  For ever quench thy fire ?
Or in thy swift, immortal race,
To gain the first archangel's place
  Wilt thou aspire ?

The Zephyr.

———

THE Queen of Night, with pensive light,
  The tranquil woods was streaking,
The roving gale on hill and dale
  Its holy thoughts was speaking :
I thought that Nature's heart was there,
And throbbing heaved the balmy air,
So calmly, gently beating were
  The pulses of the breeze.
I thought the sighing grottoes played
To woo the stars, a serenade,
As sweet as lover to his maid
  Upon their bended knees.
So soft the song, so sad the sigh,
That from their windows in the sky
The stars sent love-beams in reply
  To kiss those minstrel trees.

The sighing Zephyr seemed to be
  A spirit at my side.
I spoke to it, and thus to me
  In whispers it replied :

I am the poet of the wood,
  And bards repeat in rhyme
The songs with which in solitude
  I pass away my time.
What I have sung in Nature's tongue,
  They sing again in thine.

From thought and books I call the sage
  To groves and woodlands wild.
I waken in the breast of age
  The feelings of a child ;
And wrinkled Care and cold Despair
  I've cheered until they smiled.

From land to land, from east to west,
  I journey to and fro,
To calm awhile the troubled breast,
  And soothe the pangs of woe.
I may not stay, for ere the day
  I've many miles to go.

Music spreading, fragrance shedding
Softly as an angel treading,
  Passed the Zephyr by.
Pleasures ever, lasting never,
Though enchanting as the Zephyr,
  Like the Zephyr fly.

Morning.

THE pale night speeds in widows' weeds
  To mourn, and watch, and pray,
In hallowed gloom beside the tomb
  Of the departed Day.
While Nature sleeps she sits and weeps,
  Or sings some plaintive lay.

In twilight dressed she came and pressed
  His warm lips ere he died,
With half-drawn breath she watched his death,
  And sorrowed as his bride,
Then wrapt in shrouds of misty clouds
  His corpse, at Eventide.

From yonder sky her languid eye
  Now sheds a pensive glow,
In sighs she speaks, and down her cheeks
  The cold tears faster flow;
Yet still in prayer she lingers there,
  And scorns to hide her woe.

But now her glance can see advance
　Her infant son, the Morn,
And she can trace his father's face
　Upon his childish form.
His eye is bright, his step is light,
　And his young blood is warm.　'

Aside she throws, with all her woes,
　The mourning suit she wore,
Dispels her fears, and wipes the tears
　Which she had shed before ;
For in his child the Day has smiled
　On her in love once more.

What is Memory?

It is the consecrated ground
In which the cold remains are found
  Of thoughts once warm and gay.
Some graves are fresh, and some are green,
And some the moss has grown between,
  And some are in decay.

On one secluded, holy spot,
There blooms a wild "Forget-me-not,"
  And cypress waves above.
The heart goes often there to weep,
For in that lowly grave there sleep
  False hope and blighted love.

Whene'er we visit it, there start
From this cold graveyard of the heart,
  The spectres of the dead.
Whichever way our eyes are cast,
They meet these phantoms of the past,
  Of feelings that have fled.

The forms of pain, of crime, of care,
Of foiled ambition, of despair,
   We vainly seek to shun ;
But those of joy, of jovial youth,
Of holy deeds, of thoughts of truth,
   We welcome one by one.

When death has claimed our lifeless dust,
All these departed feelings must
   In solemn pomp arise,
To meet the spirit at the gate
That hides the disembodied state
   From view by mortal eyes.

The River.

I know a stream whose infant spring
  Is hid in a cradle of moss,
Round which the winds like muses sing
  Soft lullabies, as they toss
The curtains which the leaflets string
  By joining their hands across.

A thoughtful mind will always find
  A type in that lovely stream,
Of human life ere care and strife
  Have broken its early dream.

O'er beds of sand and pebble-stones
  The waters playfully glide,
And talk in merry laughing tones
  To the flowers on either side,
While oft a drooping primrose owns
  Their love with a kiss of pride.

So childhood steals and never feels
  A dread of approaching ill.
Its heart is light, its thoughts are bright,
  And pure as a gushing rill.

The river soon is deep and strong,
  And, proud of its giant force,
It dashes fearlessly along
  O'er cataracts in its course.
A dauntless spirit fires its song,
  Its voice is becoming hoarse.

Thus youth disdains to wear the chains
  Of prudence and self-control,
For now the swell and mystic spell
  Of passion, expand its soul.

At times the torrents swiftly flow
  In pomp, through a gorgeous wood,
Or wander seriously and slow,
  In a sullen, thoughtful mood,
Through dark ravines, or winter snow,
  Or a barren solitude.

So childhood fleets, and manhood meets
  The gloomy as well as the gay,
As fortune smiles and hope beguiles,
  Or pleasures and wealth decay.

I saw a gentle streamlet cast
  Her form on the flood to rest,
The swelling river held her fast
  As a bride upon his breast.
They flowed until they came at last
  To an ocean in the west.

Thus man at length exerts his strength
  With his young bride in his arms,
To nobly brave each troubled wave
  On the world's broad sea of storms.

Fair Maid, Hide thy Face.

FAIR MAID ! hide thy face !
 Lest the angels say
Thou art of their race,
 And must come away.

The cloud clasps the moon
 In its naked arms,
But boasts not the bloom
 Of thy fairer charms.

The moon, with a kiss,
 Bids the cloud adieu,
To find sweeter bliss
 As she kisses you.

The sun is asleep
 With his bride the sea,
Like him would I keep
 All the night with thee ;

For forest, and flower,
 And the sky above,
Say this is the hour,
 And the place of love.

And stretched at our feet
 Is the moonlight spread,
As white as a sheet,
 For our bridal bed.

Complaint of the Old Oak Tree.

I've lived to see my glory blasted,
  To watch my leaves depart,
To feel my hollow trunk has lasted
  Much longer than my heart.

My neighbours, talking to each other,
  Despise the poor old oak,
Whose limbs had, after one another,
  A paralytic stroke.

Amid the rising generation,
  Young, beautiful, and gay,
I stand in utter desolation,
  And crumble to decay.

The woodman, Death, is often taking
  Some fair and happy tree,
But though my withered hands are shaking,
  He always passes me.

Dreams.

Are dreams the echoes of our waking thought ?
  The shadows of the objects seen by day ?
The spectres of the past that rise unsought,
  Then swiftly glide away ?

Or does the soul in slumber wing its flight
  To those mysterious realms where mind is free,
And there, endowed with dim prophetic light,
  See that which is to be ?

Sleep is a great magician, whose command
  With fancied melody can charm the ear,
While dreams, like spirits from the fairy land,
  At his request appear.

His spells can make departed friends arise,
  And bid us hold communion with the dead,
Or draw down holy angels from the skies
  To hover round our bed.

But dreams may come when not invoked by sleep,
   The captive, fettered to his dungeon floor,
The faithful lover, whom the envious deep
   Parts from his native shore ;

The warrior, whose ambition grasps a throne,
   The sage, exploring wisdom's varied streams,
The bard, with fancy's paradise his own,—
   All have their waking dreams.

And what if all above, beneath, around,
   The sky, the clouds, the landscape, and the main,
With even our own bodies, should be found
   Strange fictions of the brain !

Philosophers confess they cannot tell
   Things which exist from those which only seem ;
But death at last will break the magic spell
   Of life's mysterious dream.

An Hour.

WHILE upon my couch I pondered,
And beside me Fancy wandered
　From her fairy bower,
Thus I spoke in thoughtful sadness,
With a poet's meaning madness,
　To the passing Hour.

Yonder clock is ticking loudly,
'Tis thy stout heart throbbing proudly
　In its mortal strife.
And the hand is death's cold finger,
On the Hour it seems to linger,
　Waiting for thy life.
Ere thou joinest by-gone ages
Trace thy history's varied stages,
Read its bright and sombre pages
　From the book of time.
Hark ! like viewless mourners stealing
Sound the notes thy death revealing,
For the bells thy knell are pealing
　In their midnight chime.
Bid thy spectre pass before me,
By some secret sign assure me
That thy spirit, hovering o'er me,
　Whispers unto mine.
Through my veins there ran a shiver,
And my limbs began to quiver
　With a nameless dread.
This I deemed the spirit's token,
And a voice like music spoken
　Thus in answer said :

Were I to lift the gilded screen
  And shew you what I might,
My drama of an hour would seem
The visions of a madman's dream
  Prolonged through endless night.
But in review, I will, for you,
Recall an episode or two,
  Before I take my flight.

A gambler left his dying child
  To meet the fiend of dice ;
His face was haggard, worn, and wild,
And freezing was the smile he smiled,
  As if his heart were ice.
His cheeks, once hale, were ghastly pale,
And each deep wrinkle formed a trail
  To track the steps of vice.

A drunkard laughed an idiot's laugh,
  And swore an idle boast,
While ruin, with her goblin staff,
Looked on and saw her victim quaff
  To wealth a parting toast ;
And crime stood by, with blood-shot eye,
And smiled upon her stanch ally—
  The stout and jovial host.

An old man sat, with look half weird,
  Beside a smouldering fire ;
His cheeks were wan, his eyes were bleared,
His palsied limbs were shrunk and seared,
  And clad in mean attire.
In sombre gloom around the room
His children's spectres from the tomb
  Were waiting for their sire.

Through lordly halls a noble walked,
  And muttered words and sighed.
It was not to himself he talked,
For like his own dark shadow stalked
  A phantom at his side.
His crime was known to God alone,
Yet on his arm as cold as stone
  He felt his murdered bride.

Upon the margin of a lake
  There stood a maiden fair,
No tear she wept, no word she spake,
But from her breast I saw her take
  One lock of raven hair.
The depth profound of waters round
Sent forth a sudden splashing sound,
  Then all was stillness there.

Without a priest or sexton's aid,
  A coffin, shroud, or bier,
By moonlight pale a grave was made,
And in that grave a corpse was laid,
  Though none of kin stood near,
Save only one, the dead man's son,
Who shuddered when the rite was done—
  Whose lips were blanched with fear.

A miser's haunted soul fled by
  Just when the hour bell tolled.
I watched his life's last embers die,
As death blew out each sunken eye
  And left it dark and cold.
With stifling gasp he tried to clasp
The air in his convulsive grasp,
  As if he clutched at gold.

I heard a trampling to the grave
   Each ticking of the clock.
A prince rode up, and then a slave,
And then a madman stopped and gave
   A loud impatient knock.
None had to wait, for fixed as fate
Thè porter's hand was on the gate,
   The key was in the lock.

The shade of fever seemed to haunt
   The dwellings of the poor,
While like a spectre, grim and gaunt,
The fleshless skeleton of want
   Unlatched the shattered door,
And bloated law looked in and saw
No plunder save a bed of straw
   That lay upon the floor.

I marked the plague with noiseless stealth
   All livid, worn, and thin,
Sit down beside the hearths of health,
And lurk among the halls of wealth
   To breathe its poison in.
Its watch it kept while Nature slept,
And like a pale assassin crept
   Amid a revel's din.

I traced the progress of a spark
   That shot a lurid glare.
It seemed an eye-ball in the dark,
Whose sullen flashes served to mark
   That fire was crouching there.
Within an hour that fury's power
Had wrapt in flames a palace tower,
   And scorched the midnight air.

I saw a black cloud sailing fast,
  I heard the wild winds rave.
The shrieking demon of the blast
In fiendish frolic seized a mast,
  And flung it to the wave ;
Then bade the surge burlesque a dirge
For those who stood upon the verge
  Of ocean's tombless grave.

I found a world, a book, a play,
  In every human heart,
For thoughts appeared and passed away,
And like an actor, sad or gay,
  Each passion chose its part,
While hopes forgot, or cherished not,
Like ghosts to aid or end the plot,
  Unsummoned seemed to start.

From under memory's coffin lid
  Those solemn shadows stole,
For in each breast a corpse was hid,
A haunted room locked up amid
  The chambers of the soul,—
A tale unsaid of pleasures dead,
A book of legends wild and dread
  As some ancestral scroll.

But Nature's hand would quench the sun,
  And give new planets birth,
Ere I could number, one by one,
The deeds that in an hour were done
  Upon the face of earth,
Or half disclose the joys or woes
That in each breast the life-blood froze,
  Or struck the chords of mirth.

The volume where I wrote the wrong
  That spared no race nor clime,
Was crossed, and closely lined, and long,
And smeared with blots of blood among
  Its paragraphs of crime ;
But sadly brief that half-filled leaf
That told each patriot's holy grief,
  And hero's acts sublime.

But see ! the radiant haud of day,
  In Nature's mystic scrawl,
Is writing with a golden ray
The greeting which it cannot say
  Upon the chamber wall.
I must begone, for rosy dawn
The sky's dark window blinds has drawn,
  And let night's curtains fall.

From my reverie I started,
And the phantom Hour depart d
  To its shroud, the past.
All the actors, grave or tragic,
Summoned by the spirit's magic,
  Left the stage at last,—
Left me half philosophising,
Moody, sad, soliloquising,
Into maxims theorising
  What the Hour had sung—
Left me wrapt in mystic fancies,

Dreaming dramas and romances
Such as came in waking trances
 When my heart was young.
While I write, the old clock stutters
Dirges which the church bell mutters,
And the loud cathedral utters
 With its solemn tongue.

The Deserted House.

THE ancient roof was hoary
　　With flakes of drifted snow,
And each deserted story
　　Possessed a look of woe.

Their latest guest, the spider,
　　Had left the vacant halls,
And time was rending wider
　　The fissures in the walls.

The winds alone, undaunted,
　　With sounds of mystic gloom,
Like former tenants haunted
　　Each damp and dismal room.

Thus silent, sad, and dreary,
　　Becomes the empty heart,
When all its guests grow weary,
　　And one by one depart ;

When hope's last dying flashes
　　In sullen night expire,
And age stirs out the ashes
　　Of passion's former fire.

Then memory, coldly stealing,
　　Like winter's mournful blast,
Invokes the ghost of feeling,
　　The echoes of the past.

To Ambition.

PHANTOM ! foe to pleasure !
  Stern, unbidden guest !
Leave me to my leisure !
  Let my spirit rest !
Soul of morbid sadness !
Fiend of early madness !
Chase not peace and gladness
  From my breast !

Falsely hast thou spoken
  To my trusting heart,
But thy spell is broken,
  And my dreams depart.
Childhood's hopes disown me,
Cold despair has known me,
And the world has shewn me
  What thou art.

Yet, though sorrows banish
  Youth's ambitious pride,
Though its visions vanish,
  And its smiles have died,
Still vain thoughts are flocking,
At my heart's door knocking,
And thou standest mocking
  At my side.

Love and wine and laughter
  Scare thee for a night,
But thou comest after,
  With the morrow's light,
And my heart feels older,
Sullen thoughts grow bolder,
Earth seems bleaker, colder,
  In my sight.

'Twixt my thoughts and duty,
  'Twixt my dreams and trade,
Rise dim forms of beauty,
  Starts thy scornful shade;
And my spirit soaring,
Wrapt, entranced, adoring,
Sweeps through space, imploring
  Fancy's aid.

Thus I spurn the real,
  With a fool's disdain,
Grasping the ideal,
  And its shadows vain;
Thus the world advances,
Seizing fortune's chances,
While I chase the fancies
  ' Of my brain.

Human Greatness.

LET men of genius, wealth, or place,
　Who proudly pass us by,
For symbols of their grandeur trace
Those myriads of a puny race
　That in some dewdrop lie;
For earth, with all its pomp and pride,
Is but a pebble, which the tide
Of boundless space has washed aside
　In some small creek of sky;
And those whom meaner men call great,
On whom, like slaves, dependants wait,
Are human insects robed in state,
　That mimic gods, and die.

With solemn look the tedious sage
　Parades his varied lore,
And learns from history's tragic page
What actors trod life's paltry stage
　In ages gone before;
Then racks, perhaps, his aching brains
O'er some old poet's classic strains,
And deems the universe contains
　No source of wisdom more;
While all the thoughts of all mankind,
To being's soundless sea of mind,
Are but the weeds it leaves behind
　On time's polluted shore.

'Twas not for creatures such as man,
 Who dwells in reason's night,
That life through Nature's pulses ran,
And countless worlds their march began
 Round countless orbs of light;
For surely yonder gorgeous skies
Must have some tenants pure and wise,
Whose souls, that gaze on truth, despise
 Our spirits' meaner flight,—
Who with amused contempt survey
These feeble forms of breathing clay,
That deck themselves in grand array,
 And boast of fancied might.

A Sceptic's Soliloquy on Human Ignorance.

WE love and hate, and feel the strife
    Of passions oft intense ;
We live, yet know not what is life.
    We are, but know not whence.
We talk of unknown links that bind
The mortal frame to viewless mind,
But who those mystic links can find ?
    Or prove the truth of sense ?

When countless ages shall have fled
    Will stars still deck the sky ?
And tears of anguish still be shed
    By beings born to die ?
Or will some nobler species then
From old remains judge how and when
There lived the puny race of men,
    In cycles long gone by ?

We see the torch of history cast
    A few faint streaks of light,
But these no more illume the past
    Than glow-worms light the night ;
For what, mid endless time, appears
That space of some six thousand years
Of human hopes, and joys, and tears,
    Of which historians write ?

We turn our thoughts from what has been
    To that which is to be,
And speak of realms by sense unseen,
    Where mind, we say, is free ;
Yet, though the flippant fool may prate,
And trembling sages speculate,
Still, hovering round man's future state
    Are clouds of mystery.

We ask philosophy the cause
    Which makes the planets roll,
Or bid it seek to trace the laws
    Of matter and the soul ;
We guess and doubt, we read and think,
We follow logic link by link
To nothing, at whose awful brink
    We reach vain reason's goal.

Gray Hairs:

AN OLD MAN'S LAMENT.

I CARE not for to-morrow,
For I look with shame and sorrow
  On a life time thrown away.
I have shunned all serious thinking
Till my aching brain is sinking
  Into premature decay,
Till my wan looks are revealing
That the night of age is stealing,
And my heart has grown unfeeling,
  And my hair is turning gray.

From the cup of vice I tasted,
And my youth was worse than wasted
  Mid the laughter of the gay.
Not a noble action doing,
Not a noble aim pursuing,
  I have lived from day to day;
And I wake from empty dreaming,
From a dream without a meaning,
When the past is past redeeming,
  And my hair is turning gray.

I have had my thirst for glory,
For a page in history's story,
  For a part in life's strange play,
But my heart so long has trifled
That ambition's voice is stifled,
  And I heed not what men say.
And I look on death with gladness,
For my soul is full of sadness,
And my thoughts are wild to madness,
  And my hair is turning gray.

When I cease from tears and laughter
In the vague and dim hereafter,
  And my body turns to clay,
Not a heart my fame will cherish
And my life's faint track will perish
  As a ship's on ocean's spray ;
And my grave will lie neglected,
For my name is unrespected,
Not a worthy deed effected,
  Though my hair is turning gray.

The Visionary.

A PALE youth sits; before him lies a book.
How grand the language of his earnest look !
A proud smile curls his lips, but now he sighs,
And now hope flashes from his dreaming eyes.
As one entranced, he takes the book and reads
Of mighty heroes and their deathless deeds;
Thought clouds his brow, ambition thrills his heart,
Before his gaze imagined armies start,
Earth's lightnings flash, war's thunders round him roll,
The blast of trumpets vibrates through his soul;
To death or fame he leads a dauntless band,
A visionary sword is in his hand,
He bleeds from fancied wounds, but feels not pain,
For war's sublime delirium fires his brain.
　But not of arms alone the dreamer dreams,
For oft his fancy dwells on gentler themes.
The shades of mighty bards before him stand,
Of Homer lofty and of Virgil grand,
Of Milton wrapt in thought, and Byron proud,
And god-like Shakespeare, chief among the crowd.
Then martial sounds no more his thoughts inspire,
His scorched heart feels a poet's fiercer fire,
His brow, he says, shall wear the wreath of fame,
And unborn nations learn his deathless name.

In fancy, too, he treads new fields of thought,
Reads all that priests and scholars ever taught,
Learns proud philosophy's conflicting codes,
Each problem solves, each theory explodes,
And clears the doubts which have, from age to age,
Perplexed the brain of each succeeding sage.
Then, leaving themes abstruse, his earnest mind
Exerts itself to bless and teach mankind ;
The labours of his intellect impart
New strength to science and new life to art ;
And Nature's secrets, from the world concealed;
By him possessed, to him alone revealed,
Exalt him far above each gaudy thing
That struts and rules and calls itself a king.

Wild legends, too, of alchymists of old,
Who dreamt of endless life and boundless gold,
Inspire a trembling eagerness to look
Through each unopened leaf of wisdom's book,
Whose untranslated pages would, if read,
Unfold the awful secrets of the dead,
And make vain man, with all his fancied power,
The slave and plaything of his idlest hour.

Mid hopes like these, each brighter than the last,
Through fairy realms the years of youth glide past ;
And if he seeks, in an abstracted mood,
The pensive calm of sacred solitude,
There fame, in some enchanting shape arrayed,
Pursues his steps as closely as his shade,

Throws o'er his senses so divine a spell,
Invokes such visions, makes such raptures swell,
That in his trance he deems her promised bays,—
The world's approving smile,—the scholar's praise,—
Enough, if gained, to please a spirit's pride,
And leave ambition not a thought beside.

The scene is changed: with features worn and wan
Alone at midnight sits a moody man.
No brilliant visions cheat his fancy now,
But lines of thought are traced upon his brow.
A pile of learned manuscripts and books,
Is at his side, yet not on these he looks,
But, starting from his seat, in accents low
Thus mutters sadly, pacing to and fro:

I was a madman to contend with fate,
A fool to dream of being wise or great;
For could my thoughts, in search of truth, have gained
A wider range than genius e'er attained,
Still would the meanest spirit's humblest flight
As far have passed my wisdom's utmost height,
As my own soul excels the senseless sod
Compared with which it is itself a god.
The more I learn, the less I seem to know,
The more I think, the more confused I grow,
For reason's maze contains no pathway out
Save boundless faith or universal doubt.
Perplexed with sophistries, both old and new,
Nought save my own existence now seems true,

And all that sense reveals, each sight and sound,
The very air I breathe, the world around,
Appear no longer facts, but only seem
Remembered fictions of a broken dream.
I have pursued false logic's winding track,
Till, round and round, her steps have led me back
To dreary nothing, where, as they began,
End all the vain philosophies of man.
It is an awful thing to live and die,
Yet seek in vain to fathom how or why;
To grope for truth, unaided by a spark
Of reason's fire to guide me through the dark;
To question all things, yet discover nought;
To think, yet never find out what is thought;
To study long, yet be compelled to own
My very self is to myself unknown,
And that to only this my faith extends—
I know I am, and there my knowledge ends.
I have perused the books of ancient lore,
And read the lives of empires now no more.
And yet how little is my learning worth?
For what, amid infinitude, is earth?
Throughout eternity, in boundless space,
What mighty changes must have taken place,
What myriads of new worlds their course begun,
And in those worlds how many deeds been done,
While I, whose childish vision reaches not
Beyond this little planetary spot,

Know nothing save the paltry care and strife
That fill the trivial tale of human life.
Each planet whirled through yonder awful vast
May have its tragic records of the past,
Its codes of law, its kingdoms and its crowns,
Its seas, its hills, its deserts and its towns,
Its palaces and huts, its lords and slaves,
Its young and old, its cradles and its graves.
Perchance, this moment, heedless of the crowd,
Some dreamer like myself, reserved and proud,
Despising life, yet half afraid to die,
In silence views the broad expanse of sky,
And, gazing on this little earthly sphere,
Asks whether any conscious shapes dwell here,
And thinks if so, that they at least must be
From death exempt, from pain and sadness free.
Each drop that washes earth's unmeasured strand,
Perhaps each speck of dust and grain of sand,
Are peopled worlds, where nations live and die
Invisible to man's unaided eye.
For aught I know, beyond the gaze of sense
A sky expands, whose worlds are so immense
That earth itself, to them, would be no more
Than is to earth each sand upon the shore ;
And in those worlds, if worlds so vast there are,
A race may dwell, surpassing man so far
That I, whose soul has sought for truth, should be
Less wise to them than insects are to me,

And kings and heroes by their side appear
The puny rulers of an atom sphere.
If one of that exalted race could find
The secrets of a human insect's mind,
How strange, how sadly ludicrous would seem
That human insect's philosophic dream—
Its laughable ambition to be great,
Its feeble struggles in the arms of fate,
Its reason's weak attempts to seem profound,
Its notions of the universe around,
Of space and thought, eternity and time,
Things past and future, simple and sublime.
But what to me, a creature of a day,
A worthless form of animated clay,
Are those mysterious orbs that seem to lie
In tranquil thought amid the solemn sky?
No wish nor deed of mine can change my lot,
Can give me powers which Nature gave me not,
Can turn disease and death to endless youth,
Nor burst the bars that guard the gates of truth.
Accursed Ambition! whom I called divine!
To whom I sold the heart that once was mine!
Allured with hopes of wisdom's promised goal
I cast each human passion from my soul;
And now thou laughest at my black despair,
Thy visions mock my grasp like empty air;
My brain still thinks, but all its thoughts are sad,
And if I live thy taunts will drive me mad.

More blessed is he who boasts of wealth or birth,
Whose world is self, whose universe is earth,
Than those to whom this spacious globe appears
An atom lost amid unnumbered spheres,
Who, pondering o'er illimitable space,
Despise themselves, their destiny, their race,
Yet cannot change the Nature which they scorn,
Nor mould the fate to which their liveswere born.
Then let me crush each philosophic doubt,
Put morbid passion's smouldering embers out;
Forget the stars, think not of boundless space,
And deem mankind a proud and favoured race
Whose mortal frames are caskets that enshrine
Immortal souls with powers almost divine.
Thus may I learn, by seeing nought beside,
To view my insignificance with pride,
To think each worthless toy a glorious prize,
My errors truth, my very follies wise,
My mind a sea whose billows reach no bound,
Sublime in passion, in repose profound.

    Thus spoke the dreary man, whose heart in youth
Had worshipped fame and wildly throbbed for truth.
    Grown reckless from despair, in vain he sought
To still ambition and extinguish thought,
With gay companions mingled for a while,
Compelled his lips to wear a vacant smile,
From silence shrank as from a demon's spell,
And from himself as from the bounds of hell;

But neither beauty's glance, nor song, nor jest,
Could charm the snake concealed within his breast,
And fits of gloom, like sullen shadows, stole
Between his comrades and his darkened soul.
At times a horrid phantom seemed to start,
And blanch his haggard cheek, and freeze his heart;
More ghastly than the spectres of the dead,
It tracked his steps, and stood beside his bed,
And ruled his tortured thoughts, and mocked his will,
And even in his dreams pursued him still.
From his own soul that fearful phantom came,
And Madness, morbid Madness, was its name.
In vain, by forced and hollow mirth, he tried
To see it not, or laugh it from his side ;
A horrid fascination fixed his gaze,
His dark despair assumed a darker phase,
Until at last, as one bewitched, he had
The wish, the hope, the craving to be mad.
Delirium would, he argued, lull to rest
The ghosts of blighted hopes that thronged his breast,
And from his heart, by potent spells, would force
Those lurking demons, memory and remorse.
Then let, he said, the hand of madness cast
A veil of darkness o'er the dreary past,
Let reason cease to rule my thoughts and acts,
Let truth to me seem false, and fictions facts.
The madman, who in fancy rules the globe,
Esteems his rags a monarch's stately robe,

Believes his keepers slaves, his mandates law,
And for a sceptre grandly wields a straw,
Enjoys as much as millions of the sane
Who view his pride with pity or disdain,
And more, perhaps, than some who wear a crown,
Or grasp at wealth, or struggle for renown,
Or famish for the truth, and yet confess
That logic only teaches how to guess,
That nothing is as it appears to be,
But all things lie in hopeless mystery.
Then what, he said, is madness, save a change
From life's strange dreams to others not more strange?
For who, among the whole of humankind,
Is free from some delusion of the mind?
Thus thought the morbid man : fresh seasons came
And changed the earth, but he remained the same ;
For death in mocking malice passed him by
To seize on those who had no wish to die,
And madness, though its shadow dimmed his sight,
Still left enough of reason's hated light
To throw a kind of cold and sickly glare
Around the ghastly visions of despair.
   It was a sultry eve : his brow was hot
With burning fever, yet he knew it not,
Nor heeded that his limbs were parched and weak,
Nor felt the fire that preyed upon his cheek,
But wandered forth until he reached a rock
Whose rough and scowling summit seemed to mock

The mumbling surges rolling to and fro
In sullen wrath a hundred feet below.
At intervals there came a lurid flash,
And now and then, above the wild waves' splash,
He heard the words the volleyed thunder spoke
In hoarse and angry tones, as if they broke
From some offended god, whose soul had grown
As weary of existence as his own.
Awhile he stood and gazed; then o'er him came
The terror of a spell without a name,
It drew him on, it urged him to the brink,
He only felt its power, he could not think,
It numbed his senses with a death-like chill,
It fixed his eyes on the abyss, until
His brain grew dizzy and his sight grew dim,
And o'er his heart and through each quivering limb
A tremor ran, an icy shudder crept,
And nought of consciousness remained, except
That thirst for life, though life be void of hope,
Which seldom quits the darkest misanthrope.
His spell was broken by a fearful blast
Of volleyed thunder, louder than the last,
That rent the sky until it died among
The scowling clouds, like snatches of a song
Of madness and revenge, whose fierce notes hurled
Undying hate and scorn from world to world.
Its solemn tones, its deep and hollow roll,
Woke scornful echoes in his gloomy soul;

And seemed to mock the fear which made him crave
To hated life, when, if he could but brave
An instant's pang, his wearied frame might be
A mangled corpse beneath the surging sea.
One fatal moment, if he could but dare,
A single step, a falling through the air,
A cry of agony, a gasp for breath,
And then the blank or mystery of death.
One foot he raised, one nervous look he cast,
But paused to think, and then shrank back aghast.
Again he neared the brink, again looked o'er,
But paused again, and shuddered as before,
Then closed his eyes, advanced a step or two,
And fell, but falling clutched a shrub that grew
O'erhanging the abyss ; he tried to speak,
But terror froze his tongue ; at length a shriek,
A frenzied cry of anguish and despair,
One half a curse, one half a demon's prayer,
Burst from his lips, but ere its sound had died
An answer came, a distant voice replied.
He shuddered still, but hope was mixed with fear,
He might be saved, for human aid was near,
Again he shrieked, the voice replied again,
His blood ran cold, truth flashed across his brain,
For from no human lips that answer broke,
But mocking echo was the fiend who spoke.
When morning dawned, among the wild rocks lay
A mangled corpse, a mass of shapeless clay :
Thus closed the life of him, whose morbid mind
Aspired to pass the bounds of humankind,
Presumed to search for truths by man unknown,
And envy natures nobler than his own.

The Hermit.

———

UNFAMED as hero, bard, or sage,
   And yet in secret proud,
A hermit lived, whose hermitage
   Was life's unthinking crowd.
For though at times his lips might jest,
His cloistered soul, despising rest,
Kept mumbling thoughts within his breast
   Which were not said aloud.

His friends, who heard the words he spoke,
   Believed him light as they,
For oft, with wine and song and joke,
   He laughed swift hours away;
Yet none could guess what visions beamed,
What thoughts he thought, what dreams he dreamed,
What passions thrilled him, while he seemed
   So blithe and free and gay.

Thus like a Hermit dwelt his heart,
   Its inner life unknown,
Amid the world, and yet apart,
   Surrounded, yet alone;
With scarce an earthly care or aim,
A wish for wealth, a hope of fame,
A friend whose joys or griefs could claim
   Communion with its own.

A Day with the Dead.

Who would not bear an age of woe,
  Or fling a crown away,
To leave his earthly frame below,
And know what only spirits know,
  For but a single day,—
To gaze on death, to pierce the gloom
That hides the secrets of the tomb,
And then, once more a man, resume
  His cast-off robes of clay.

How far beneath his scorn would seem
  The fame so fiercely sought,
The mad fanatic's grandest scheme,
The scholar's lore, the poet's dream,
  With all that books e'er taught,—
To him whose mortal part had died,
Whose soul had drawn death's veil aside,
Had felt a spirit's power and pride
  And boundless range of thought.

Three Score Years and Ten.

WHILE hoping, laughing, weeping,
Dull age is softly creeping,
　As months and years roll by,
And life, however extended,
In death so soon is ended,
That time is best expended
　In learning how to die.

The merchant, shrewdly trading,
Thinks meanness not degrading,
　Nor scruples at a lie.
When wealth, at last, brings leisure,
Too old for love or pleasure,
He looks upon his treasure,
　And lays him down to die.

The student, riches spurning,
Beholds the book of learning,
　Whose leaves are earth and sky,
And, like the wisest sages
Of other climes and ages,
Just opes the mystic pages,
　Then shuts them up, to die.

Were centuries before us,
Ere age, first stealing o'er us,
　　Could dim youth's flashing eye,
Fame might be worth the craving,
And wealth the toil of slaving,
And man have time for saving,
　　And time to live and die.

But what is rank or glory
To him whose hair is hoary,
　　Whose life's last moments fly?
And what can power avail us
When health and vigour fail us,
When death's swift darts assail us,
　　And clothed in pomp we die.

The Dreamer.

———

Shunning facts, and shadows grasping,
Dreams the dreamer, phantoms clasping,
   Wearing fancied bays.
Hoping, scheming, thinking, dreaming,
Rapture, faith, or frenzy gleaming
   From his restless gaze.

Now in silent thought he ponders,
Now with look abstracted wanders
   Through some sylvan scene,
Weaves romances from his fancies,
Scorn's the world's most brilliant chances,
   Counts its grandeur mean.

Fortune shuns the idle schemer,
And the dreamings of the dreamer
   Vanish like his breath,
Changing gladness into sadness,
Causing morbid hate, or madness,
   Or an early death.

The Recluse;

OR, MORBID AMBITION.

———

No friends he sought, no precepts taught,
For his soul was wrapt in silent thought,
   And the world he heeded not ;
Yet none so rude as would intrude
On his dark or holy solitude,
   In a drear, deserted spot.
The storm-fiend woke, the thunder spoke,
And the tempest rent the stalwart oak,
When a sound of words in murmur's broke
   From his lone and lowly cot.

Why did I madly seek to find
The laws of disembodied mind :
To learn those secrets, dark, sublime,
Deemed magic in the olden time :
To be what man has never been,
Survey that realm by sense unseen,
Invoke the dead, and bid them show
The wisdom none but spirits know ?
Why was I racked with hopes and pride
So vast as this, and yet denied
The strength of soul, the power of thought,
To grasp the truths thus vainly sought ?
Yet earth and air and sea abound
With secrets deep, with thoughts profound,

And reason ne'er suggests a doubt
That, could I find those secrets out,
Men's lives would hang upon my breath,
My skill would make me laugh at death,
Perhaps give power to stop decay,
Mould living forms from senseless clay,
And lend my name such fearful awe
That states would own my mandates law.
The chemist has but learned to look
Through one short page of Nature's book,
Yet even he, though far from wise,
Can draw down lightnings from the skies,
Make simplest things strange wonders tell,
Dissolve, as by a wizard's spell,
Turn holy love to raging lust,
The breathing form to lifeless dust,
Give reason's eye a vacant stare,
Or bid it flash with frenzy's glare,
Obscure the mind that lights an age,
And to an idiot change the sage.
But what is all the chemist's skill,
His boasted arts for good or ill,
With all the wisdom books disclose,
And all that science thinks she knows,
Compared with what my power would be
Were half I seek revealed to me?
If on this brow there sat a crown,
In utter scorn I'd cast it down,
And bear a thousand years of pain,
Could I at such a cost obtain
A glimpse at those strange truths that lie,
Those worlds unseen by mortal eye,
Within as much of air or land
As might be grasped within this hand,

For in each atom would be shewn
A world as yet to man unknown.
　　Do spirits, though I know not how,
In scorn or pity watch me now,
And know the thoughts that o'er me steal,
And what I hope and think and feel?
Is there no secret path between
The world of sense and world unseen,
By which the disembodied can　'
Return and talk with mortal man?
No way, save death, by which my soul
May spurn this body's dull control,
And know and feel, for one short hour,
A spirit's knowledge, will, and power?
In olden time a wizard's spell
Was thought to reach the depths of hell,
And make appear, with noiseless tread,
The ghastly phantoms of the dead,
And bid their bloodless lips relate
The future dark decrees of fate.
Each ivied castle, too, can boast
Its haunted room and ancient ghost,
Its tale where murder, long concealed,
By fleshless witnesses revealed,
Without an outward sign or trace
Was hunted to its hiding place.
Yet, though the wizard's mystic art
Ne'er made obedient phantoms start,
And spectres of the murdered dead
May haunt no dark assassin's bed,
The diembodied souls may still,
For ought I know, have power, at will,
Some strange, material shape to wear,
As swift as light, as free as air,

And thus return and talk once more
With friends and foes they knew of yore.
The shallow sage, the learned fool,
Who thinks by some pedantic rule,
May treat as weak and false and vain
Whate'er distracts his feeble brain,
But he whose soul for wisdom looks
Beyond the science gained from books,
Deems Nature's simplest fact and change
Profoundly dark, sublimely strange,
Yet nought impossible, which thought
Has dreamed or fancied, hoped or sought.
If spirits hear what mortals say,
Then, be the hazard what it may,
In any shape it may assume,
I pray some spectre from the tomb,
Some soul whose body dwelt on earth,
Or being not of mortal birth,
Or one, if such there be, who fell
From highest heaven to lowest hell,
To meet me face to face, and speak
Some fragments of the truths I seek,
Tell how to rule, destroy, create,
To conquer that which men call fate,
And mould the world, for good or ill,
In meek subservience to my will.
No shapes appear ! no phantoms rise !
No mystic voice to mine replies !
My words go forth like empty air !
The dead can hear no mortal's prayer !
Or if they hear, in mute disdain
They let me breathe my prayer in vain !

Why do I still attempt to clasp
Dim shadows that elude my grasp?
Why linger in this dreary spot,
My very name almost forgot,
Aspiring to be more than man,
To fathom truths no mortal can,
Yet spurning all the useful lore
Which made its teachers famed of yore?
Why not confess my hopeless schemes
A morbid madman's waking dreams,
And mid the world's unceasing strife
Turn actor on the stage of life?

To drown the past, why may not I,
Like sages famed in times gone by,
Weave coils of thought to puzzle men,
Call them philosophy, and then
So darkly as to seem profound,
With bold, blaspheming words expound
What all things are, and why, and whence,
And were, and will be ages hence,
With darkest problems that relate
To God, myself, free-will, and fate,
The dead, the spirits, humankind,
Dull matter, and the realms of mind?
The very thought of fame inspires
The warrior's breast with martial fires,
And makes the wildest passions start
Within the youthful dreamer's heart.
With equal power the phantom rules
The good and bad, wise men and fools,
Throws o'er the bard its fatal spell,
Sits brooding in the hermit's cell,
Incites the grave divine to preach
With pompous air and learned speech,

Half fills the madhouse, crowds the grave,
Makes heroes reckless, cowards brave,
Leads some to virtue, more to crime,
A few to thoughts and deeds sublime,
Oft ruins empires, moulds an age,
And darkens history's fairest page.

I have not gained the ends I sought,
But much I know which is not taught,
And in that vain pursuit of truth
Which made my heart grow old in youth,
I found, beyond the chemist's lore,
Some wonders unrevealed before,
By which I might deceive the crowd,
And seem, to some at least, endowed
With something more than human skill,
And more than human power of will.
Impostors, poor and humbly born,
Fit themes for only mirth or scorn,
Have mocked at science, laughed at law,
Ruled millions with religious awe,
From haughty kings their sceptres hurled,
And changed the aspect of the world.
Let me, like them, myself proclaim
One more than man in mortal frame,
A lofty spirit come to share
A mortal's life of toil and care,
Or some departed hero's shade
In human form again arrayed,
To man commissioned to relate
The secrets of the future state.
Yet, should the daring scheme succeed,
Should prostrate nations own my creed,
Should priests expound, and men adore,
This would but make me scorn the more

Myself as false, my dupes as fools,
Whose faith each bold impostor rules ;
And still would flame that fierce desire
For hidden truth, whose quenchless fire
Burns through my soul and leaves a track
Of ashes there, all waste and black.
  Here, then, unloved, unfamed, unseen,
'Mid dreams of what I would have been,
My steps shall glide in that strange trance
Which men call life, until, perchance,
The dreamings of my soul assume
The change of madness or the tomb.
No friend shall hear my parting sigh ;
Alone I've lived, alone will die,
Unwept, unaided, gasp for breath,
And learn in silence what is death.

Madness.

———

WHAT art can cure, what skill explain,
Each strange disease that racks the brain ?
Or where is one among the sane
   From madness wholly free ?
For though the sage, with soul refined,
May scorn the maniac's darkened mind,
Their madness differs but in kind,
   And feature, and degree ;
And spirits, did they deign to speak,
Would call our wisest acts more weak,
More vain the grandest aims we seek,
Than does the idiot's idlest freak
   To us appear to be.

In one, the mania bids him trace
The lineage of his ancient race,
As if his sires were lords of space,
   And older than the sun.
To eager crowds a second shows
His frenzied rhyme or dreary prose,
And deems all conscious being knows
   The fame his works have won.

A third as proudly grasps a crown,
Or moulds a state, or rules a town,
And scowls in scorn as grandly down,
As if creation feared his frown,
   Or cared what he had done.

And what are all the systems taught
By those whose studious minds have sought
The source of matter, life, and thought,
   Save mad, fantastic schemes ?
And what each *human* creed, at best,
But some impostor's solemn jest,
Or lie in holy language drest,
   Or farce on sacred themes ?
For how can man to godhead soar,
Read being's darkest secrets o'er,
And vague infinitude explore,
When of himself he knows no more
   Than that he thinks, or dreams ?

For aught we know, all science, too,
Is but a phantom men pursue,
For whether sense be false or true
   No science yet has shewn ;
And, could our senses change, we might
Reverse the laws of sound and sight
Till night were day, and darkness light,
   And silence had a tone.

Vast worlds in yonder depth profound
May now with conscious shapes abound,
Who judge the universe around
By neither sight, nor touch, nor sound,
  But by a sense unknown.

Thus, though at morn sleep's visions break,
We seem, and only seem, to wake,
For truth has never dawned to shake
  Life's slumber from the soul.
And though these strange illusions may
At death, perchance, be chased away,
And reason, like returning day,
  Assert her lost control ;
Yet, while we live, no art nor spell
Can e'er the human madness quell
Of mind in matter's darkened cell,
Nor shew the true from false, nor tell
  The path to wisdom's goal.

Sad Thoughts;

OR,

LIFE FROM A SCEPTICAL POINT OF VIEW.

———

'TIS sad to feel oneself the slave
 Of time and sense and fate,
Yet never cease to idly crave
 For something vaguely great;
For something vast, but undefined;
Some more than mortal power of mind,
Or secret hid from human kind
 In this ignoble state.

'Tis sad to mark the scornful might
 Of rivers rushing by,—
To feel the sacred pomp of night
 When breezes softly sigh,—
To hear the thunder's hollow crash,
The tempest's howl, the wild waves' splash,
Or watch the lurid lightnings flash
 Athwart the spacious sky;

And yet to be a thing of nought,
 A creature formed of clay,—
To bear the load of sordid thought
 From dreary day to day,—
To mourn the impotence of man,
His brightest dream, some paltry plan,
His future dark, his days a span,
 His life a slow decay.

Solitude.

I WOULD a wish could place me
  In some romantic scene,
Where friend nor foe could face me,
  But deserts stretch between ;—
Where all is grand and lonely,
Where Nature liveth only,
  Where man has never been.

Thus might I, for a season,
  Break habit's dreary round,
And live where human reason
  A haunt has never found ;—
Where word was never spoken,
Nor Nature's silence broken
  By any human sound.

A Remembered Spot.

I TROD this spot in years gone by,
And yet in truth it was not I,
  But some one ceased to be ;
For not a thought remains the same,
Nor atom of my earthly frame,
Nor aught beside, except my name,
  Which is no part of me.

The youth who stood here once was fair,
And firm of step, and void of care,
  And proud, and strong, and gay ;
But time has past, and he is dead,
And now an old man in his stead,
With wrinkled hair and hoary head,
  Sits down and thinks to-day.

The Pedant.

Who would not rather choose to be
A learned fop, from sadness free,
  Of vain and feeble mind,
Than have the strength of soul to soar
Above all superficial lore
To heights of thought which ne'er before
  Were reached by humankind?
For while the shallow pedant seems
To grasp with ease the grandest themes,
And nought too darkly hidden deems
  For human skill to find,
The deeper sage, the more he knows,
In wisdom's wealth the poorer grows,
For Reason, every step she goes,
Some tinselled piece of learning throws
  As spurious coin behind.

An Atom.

Who heeds the dust that strews the ground,
Or stops to think that ought profound
　　Can in an atom lie?
Yet, could one speck its tale unfold,
Ere half the wondrous truth were told
New systems might succeed the old,
　　In yonder starlit sky.

How many times since Adam's birth,
In tree and flower this grain of earth
　　Perchance has lived and died;
And lived and died, and lived again,
In woods or fields, on hill or plain,
In human form, or grass or grain,
　　Or countless shapes beside.

Let science say what cycles past
Before this globe was doomed at last
　　To be the haunt of man;
And yet this atom filled a space
Through cycles more than sages trace,
Long ere the short-lived human race
　　Its brief career began.

Successive Creations.

———

WHAT matter though, from yonder sky,
Some wandering comet, flaming by,
Should scorch the very ocean dry,
And all that breathes in torture die
  Beneath its burning breath ?
Or if in earth's convulsive throes,
The fire that in her centre glows
Should rend the solid rocks, and close
Life's mad burlesque of pompous shows,
Of paltry cares, and joys and woes,
  In universal death ?

What though the great Unknown, in ire,
Should wrap a million worlds in fire,
And, victims on the awful pyre,
A race should in each world expire,
  Each race as proud as man ?
Or matters universal frame,
With all the conscious shapes that claim
Its countless spheres, were robed in flame,
Or sunk to nothing, whence they came,
And silence infinite should reign
  As ere the worlds began ?

Still, thronged with conscious life, as erst
From empty nothing came the first
So might a new Creation burst
With worlds of bliss, or worlds accurst,
   In each a varied race.
Yet, to the realms of boundless thought,—
Those realms with darkest mystery fraught
Of which we dream, 'twould matter nought,
Though human forms had ne'er been wrought,
Nor atoms into systems brought,
   Nor planets hurled in space.

A Dewdrop.

———

Yonder dewdrop, mimic ocean !
  To a leaflet clings,
And its waves are set in motion
  By an insect's wings ;
Yet, as science dimly traces,
In its depths that drop embraces
Crowded kingdoms, various races,
  Worlds of wondrous things.

Doubtless, too, undreamt of legions,
  Infinitely small,
Gaily, o'er its curious regions,
  Swim or fly or crawl,
Deemed by some proud dewdrop nation
Atoms mid a vast Creation,
As, from man's more lordly station,
  Atoms seem they all.

Who can tell what joy or anguish
  Those weak creatures know ?
Who can tell what myriads languish,
  Life's tide ebbing low ?
Who a dewdrop's wealth can measure,
Guess its secrets, count its treasure,
Paint its scenes of pomp and pleasure,
  Passion, pain, and woe ?

Giant souls may have a dwelling,
 Reason's fire may flame,
Thoughts sublime be grandly swelling,
 In the meanest frame ;
And, though frail the dewdrop yonder,
Puny sages there may ponder,
Puny tourists o'er it wander,
 Seeking truth or fame.

Doubtless all those studious creatures
 Deem their dewdrop, space ;
And themselves, in mind and features,
 Being's noblest race.
Dreams may come, with fancies crowded,
Of a future vague and clouded,
Of a Cause whom darkly shrouded
 In their world they trace.

But who heeds the grave opinions,
 Whether false or true,
Held within the small dominions
 Of a drop of dew ?
Who would read the tragic story
Of its tyrants grim and gory,
Of its wars and wrongs and glory,
 Strange as man e'er knew ?

Mystic dewdrop ! world of wonder !
  Empires thrive in thee !
Yet thou canst be rent asunder,
  By a breath from me !
Though thy kings be feared and. flattered,
At my touch convulsed and shattered,
In a thousand fragments scattered,
  Would their kingdoms be.

Yet 'twere vain with pride unbounded
  Of my power to boast,
Since this globe, by space surrounded,
  Seems a drop at most.
Beings, too, may somewhere flourish,
Who, as we bid dewdrops perish,
Us could crush, with all we cherish,
  Earth, with all its host.

The Hated Wind.

WITHOUT, the dull rain splashes,
 The hoarse winds wildly roar;
Within, the smouldering ashes
Throw fitful dream-like flashes,
 Athwart my study floor.
I hate this storm, that lashes
 The brawny oaks once more,
As ocean foams and clashes
 Against the rock-bound shore.
I hate it as it crashes
 Some bough I climbed of yore,
Or tears and twists and gashes
 The old thatch, patched before,—
As round the walls it dashes,
Till each cracked pane it smashes,
And shakes the window sashes,
 And strains the creaking door.

Oh wind! mad desperado?
 I hate thy scornful might,
Thy reckless, rough bravado,
Thy tempest and tornado,
 Thy howl by day and night.

At times a thoughtful langour,
  Strange maniac of the sky !
Subdues thy frenzied anger,
  And makes thee sadly sigh,
As oft, for some brief season,
There comes a flash of reason
  To madmen, ere they die.
But soon the fit comes o'er thee,
  Thy voice grows stern and high,
The forests quail before thee,
  The clouds in tumult fly,
And playing some wild antic,
Or turning fiercely frantic,
Or bound for the Atlantic,
  Thou rushest raving by.

Oft, too, I hear thee moaning,
  Like one in mental pain,
As though by prayer atoning
  For crimes on land and main,
As though by conscience taunted,
By all the spectres haunted
  Of those whom thou has slain ;
For foully thou has ridden
  O'er fertile hill and plain,
With death beside thee hidden,
  With famine in thy train,
With plagues and fell diseases
Upon thy poisoned breezes,
And withering blight that seizes
  The fields of waving grain.

Unmoved by fear or pity,
　Unawed by priest or crown,
Thou mockest at a city,
　Or howlest through a town,
Or o'er a valley rushest,
And into ruins crushest
　The cot of some poor clown.
But most, mid foaming surges,
　When clouds like demons frown,
Thou lov'st to chant old dirges,
　And mark brave ships go down,—
To watch how child and mother
In sinking clutch each other,
How brother clings to brother,
　And mock them as they drown.

Since first thy voice was sounded,
　Since winds to seas replied,
Proud cities have been founded
　Where beasts of prey now hide;
Ten thousand kings have flourished,
And men in millions perished,
　And lakes been formed and dried.
Slow masses hast thou mumbled,
　Soft anthems hast thou sighed,
O'er temples that have crumbled,
　O'er empires that have died.
Grand odes thou oft has spoken
　To some old arch, half broken,
The sole remaining token
　Of regal pomp and pride.

O wind, thou must be weary
   Of wandering to and fro,
O'er landscapes bright and dreary,
   Mid frost, and heat, and snow,—
An outlaw, homeless, friendless,
Thy journey rough and endless,
   Each living thing thy foe.
It must be dull to mutter
   The same sad wail of woe,
Which thou wast doomed to utter
   When storms were taught to blow,—
To be the same words singing,
   The same quaint music flinging,
That through the woods were ringing
   Six thousand years ago.

The Sleeping City.

So STILL the sleeping city seems,
  That but for now and then a tread,
We might forget it only dreams,
  And dream it really dead.

And when to-morrow's bells shall chime,
Could I its sleep prolong at will,
It hardly could be deemed a crime
  To bid it slumber still ;—

To bid it sleep, till grass should grow
  On spots once thronged by human feet,
And autumn winds the seed should blow
  O'er each untrodden street ;

Till one by one the roofs should fall,
  And heaven's wild storms and lightning fire
Should fling to earth each crumbling wall,
  And rend each tottering spire ;

Till moss should clothe the scattered stones,
  And hoarded coins be thick with rust,
And time should turn the very bones
  Of those who slept, to dust.

Embers.

I SAT ALONE, one dark night in December,
Till quaintly morbid fancies o'er me stole;
For in my waking dream each glowing ember
   Appeared a human soul.

'Twas strange to mark those silent, flickering ashes
Gleam out on death, and one by one expire,
To sit and watch the ghastly looks and flashes
   Of that expiring fire.

'Twas strange to think some fellow man was dying
   For each red ember smouldering at my side,—
That in some house a human corpse was lying,
   For each faint spark that died.

A Dream.

—

I HAD A DREAM, and in that dream I thought
　The sun and stars, the countless worlds that roll,
Were conscious beings, each with feeling fraught,
　Endowed with sense and will, and majesty of soul.

And orb with old orb conversed, by means of light,
　That bore, as on a mystic book, the trace
Of past and present, and, in matchless flight,
Flashed thought and knowledge round, throughout the realms
　　of space.

But o'er each stately world there crept a swarm
　Of curious insects, men among the rest,
That seemed like specks of dust, so small their form,
　Yet in those puny forms some sense of life possessed.

In pity more than mirth each conscious sphere
　Beheld these insects born, and swept away,
For in its own sublimely vast career
　A million human lives were but a single day.

Decayed Genius.

AMONG the mighty fabrics laid
  'Neath ruin's ruthless ban,
With mournful awe I once surveyed
  The ruins of a man.

The eyes that erst with genius beamed
  Had then a listless stare,
And on the vacant cheek there seemed
  Worse blankness than despair.

For save when memory's echoes woke,
  Or fancy's phantoms stole,
No thought the empty silence broke
  Throughout the darkened soul.

Vague dreams, like some old ivied wall,
  Alone remained behind,
To mark that saddest wreck of all,—
  A wrecked and ruined mind ;

And he whose words had charmed an age,
  Whose lips breathed sense and wit,
Could quote no sentence, read no page
  Of what himself had writ.

Summer and Winter.

WHEN skies are bright, and fields are green,
And balmy zephyrs fan the scene,
   And birds their love notes sing,
I love to dream each plant and tree
The sound can hear, the sight can see,
With hope's wild joy can throb like me,
   And feel the breath of spring ;

That nature loves her new attire,
And flowers each other's charms admire,
   And gushing fragrance drink ;
That streams are conscious while they flow,
And hills and vales with rapture glow,
And winds their own grand language know,
   And breathe the thoughts they think.

But when the wintry blast howls by,
And storms like spectres haunt the sky,
   And clouds drop sleet and rain ;
When trees are shivering, cold and bare,
And heaven and earth an aspect wear
Of haggard fear and dark despair,
   Of weary want and pain,—

I then could wish one mystic word
Of mine, o'er man and beast and bird
   Could spread the shroud of death,—
In each warm vein the blood could chill,
And quench each eye, and numb each will,
And bid the world's sad heart be still,
   And hush each suffering breath.

Age and Youth.

How strangely odd a thing 'twould be,
  Yet oft how sad, forsooth,
If shrivelled age could sometimes see
  The phantom of its youth;

If he who totters, worn and weak,
  With solemn silver hair,
And shrunken eye, and hollow cheek,
  And forehead ploughed with care,

Could view some smiling, dreaming face,
  Lit up with hope and health,
And in the proud young features trace
  His own departed self,

Could wake the passions, wild and deep,
  The thoughts, and joys, and fears,
That in the silent coffins sleep
  Of intervening years.

With quivering lips, the faded beau
  A ghastly smile would frame,
And on his heart's cold hearth would glow,
  A moment's flickering flame.

The bard, himself outlived, at sight
  Of what he was, would find
Again the flash of genius light
  The midnight of his mind.

The prelate bland, with smile serene,
  And pomp of pious pride,
Would blush to think he e'er had been
  The scapegrace at his side.

The felon's demon face once more
  A human look would wear,
And down upon his dungeon floor
  His knees might bend in prayer.

Oh ! what a change would oft be made,
  What smouldering fires would rage,
At sight of youth's mysterious shade,
  Within the breast of age.

The Watch Run Down.

'TIS sometimes sad to think no human power
  Can put life's timpiece back a single breath,
Can bid the pulse not tick for one brief hour,
  And steal that hour from death ;

That art, with all its boasted skill, can find,
  When age has once unwound the mystic chain,
No key to fit the watch, no way to wind
  The still works up again.

And this great globe itself, at some fixed date,
  Must change to what it was ere worlds began,
Must reach the final moment doomed by fate,
  Must run down, too, like man.

We seem to hear the solemn tick that tells
  Each circuit of the mighty wheels of time,
As through the midnight air the new year bells
  Ring out their annual chime.

And yet we know not what the clock struck last,
  But vaguely can we guess the age of earth,
Or when the hands, throughout the misty past,
  Have marked a cycle's birth.

Nor can we say how many hours remain,
  How many cycles more this orb shall see,
Ere Nature sinks to chaos back again,
  Ere time shall cease to be.

Unuttered Thoughts.

Who has not known bright thought-clouds soar,
Whose vague immensity no more
    In words compressed could be,
Than some poor artists's streaks of light,
And clumsy daubs of blue and white,
Can mirror forth the star-lit night,
    Or surging, soundless sea ?

Who has not felt, as some rich train
Of thoughts and fancies crossed his brain,
    His soul with rapture thrill,
And when they vanished, sighed to find,
Like friends who die, they left behind
A vacant place within the mind,
    No other thoughts could fill ?

For though, in memory's album bound,
Their photographs awhile are found,
    No life is in their look ;
And when, in weary, worn-out age,
These bygone dreams our thoughts engage,
So dim they seem on memory's page,
    We sadly close the book.

Endless Youth.

Must being's awful mysteries remain
　　For ever veiled in doubt ?
The simplest fool can quench life's flickering flame,
And will no genius learn to light again
　　Its fire, when once gone out ?

Is there no way to make the still heart beat ?
　　The empty lungs draw breath ?
The stagnant blood once more its course repeat ?
The stiffened corpse fling off its winding sheet,
　　And grimly laugh at death ?

Is there no mighty secret hid away,
　　Perchance for future sage ?
No herb or drug to keep us from decay ?
To stop our growing deaf, and blind, and gray ?
　　To even cure old age ?

How strange 'twould be should science yet explain
　　These uncut leaves of truth !
Should some poor scholar, great in heart and brain,
Learn how to conquer death, and banish pain,
　　And purchase endless youth !

Old men to him in eager crowds would flock,
　　And he, with scornful pride,
Might in his breast the priceless secret lock,
And watch the ages gliding on, and mock
　　The nations as they died.

Or should he teach the world his mystic lore,
　　And men still multiply,
Earth's streets in time would stretch from shore to shore,
And those who sought immortal life before,
　　Would seek the power to die.

Hidden Truths.

———

For half the ills we human dupes endure
There lies, within our reach, some simple cure,
　Not found, through want of skill ;
And one wise man, could he the truth unfold,
Might change the world, do more than seers foretold,
Our customs, creeds, and laws, though ages old,
Like flimsy cobwebs sweep away, and mould
　Our lives and thoughts at will.

We make machines that like obedient slaves
Do half our work, bear freights o'er foaming waves,
　Or plough the stubborn soil ;
But what if science at a stride could now
Advance a thousand years, and teach us how
To wipe the sweat from Labour's wrinkled brow,
Make life worth living, time for thought allow,
　And end unthinking toil.

Results more grand than sage, or seer, or bard
In dreams e'er saw, would be his vast reward
　Who hidden truth revealed,
For such an one could walk the rough world through,
And make it what he would, in moments do
The work of ages, life's short lease renew,
Extinguish pain, point out the false from true,
　And show strange things concealed.

A drug can make a maniac of the sage,
And nature's book, in some unopened page,
　　Has secrets which, if found,
Would cure the mad, give tenfold strength to thought,
And so expand men's minds that creeds now taught
As philosophic lore, would then seem nought
. Save shallow whims of babbling idiots, fraught
　　With pompous words and sound.

A Vision.

I LOOKED on a maiden's fair face,
   And her eyes for a moment met mine,
And her form was all beauty and grace,
   Like an exquisite poem in rhyme ;
And her bosom 'twas madness to trace,
As it heaved the soft folds of the lace,
   To the throbs of my heart keeping time.

The Electric Telegraph.

WHAT madman dreamt, an age ago,
   That 'neath old ocean's roar
Men's thoughts would travel to and fro,
   From distant shore to shore ?

And, though the fancy now seems strange,
   'Tis not more mad to say
That worlds may yet their news exchange
   In some undreamt of way.

Perhaps before a million years
   Their wreck-strewn course have rolled,
A million million distant spheres
   With earth will converse hold.

But whether light the means shall be,
   Or something subtler still,
Or mind at length shall learn to free
   Itself from sense at will ;

Or whether spirits, roaming space,
   Shall tidings bear about,
Are questions some much later race
   Than man, must fathom out.

The Thoughts of the Dead:

A HEATHEN PHILOSOPHER'S QUERIES.

———

WHAT become of the thoughts of the dead ?
   Do they live all eternity through ?
When our spirits from time shall have fled
   Will our lives, like a shadow, go too ?

Or of memory wrecked shall we start
   On the sands of the infinite shore ?
From the past, like a robe, shall we part
   At the threshold of death's opened door ?

If the knowledge we gain upon earth,
   Though it slumbers, can never be lost,
Then a truth is a thousand times worth
   All the toil of a life it may cost ;

But hereafter, in being's next stage,
   Any stage after this should there be,
If the fool is as wise as the sage,
   And the mind from its habits is free,

What a volume of satire is life ?
   What a farce are its hopes and its schemes,
And its friendships, and triumphs, and strife,
   And its faiths, and its facts, and its dreams !

Logic.

WITH stern philosophy I've flung aside
   Whatever was not proved, and there is nought
By reason left unchallenged, undenied,
   Except my present thought.

And yet 'tis hard to think that all I seem
   To hear and feel and taste and touch and see,
Is but a myth, a phantasy, a dream,—
   That nothing is, save me.

'Tis hard to think that space, the world, mankind,
   The breath I breathe, and Nature's works and laws,
Are but ideas, parts of my own mind,
   That come, but have no cause.

Yet so it is, for how, through fancied sense,
   Itself a dream, can truth its shadow fling,
Or how can thought, which comes I know not whence,
   Prove any outward thing?

Then I am God, and infinite. The past
   Is but a part of me. I cannot die.
Can this be true? No, reason shrinks aghast,
   And spurns the awful lie.